WHERE'S MAY?

Corey and Jasmine ran straight to Macaroni's stall. Empty!

"Macaroni's gone!" exclaimed Jasmine in dismay.

"Oh no!" cried Corey at the same time.

The two of them stared at one another. "Maybe," said Jasmine very slowly, "May couldn't get over what happened this morning. Maybe she wanted to get away."

"What are you saying?" asked Corey. "Do you think May has run away from home?"

Pony Tails

May's
Runaway Ride

BONNIE BRYANT

Illustrated by Marcy Ramsey

A SKYLARK BOOK
NEW YORK • TORONTO • LONDON • SYDNEY • AUCKLAND

RL 3, 007–010
MAY'S RUNAWAY RIDE
A Bantam Skylark Book / October 1997

Skylark Books is a registered trademark of Bantam Books,
a division of Bantam Doubleday Dell Publishing Group, Inc.
Registered in U.S. Patent and Trademark Office and elsewhere.
Pony Tails is a registered trademark of Bonnie Bryant Hiller.
"USPC" and "Pony Club" are registered trademarks of The
United States Pony Clubs, Inc., at The Kentucky Horse Park,
4071 Iron Works Pike, Lexington, KY 40511-8462.

ISBN 0-553-48484-2

Published simultaneously in the United States and Canada.

Bantam Books are published by Bantam Books, a division of Bantam
Doubleday Dell Publishing Group, Inc. Its trademark, consisting of the
words "Bantam Books" and the portrayal of a rooster, is Registered in
U.S. Patent and Trademark Office and in other countries. Marca
Registrada. Bantam Books, 1540 Broadway, New York, New York
10036.

PRINTED IN THE UNITED STATES OF AMERICA

OPM   0 9 8 7 6 5 4 3 2 1

*I would like to give my special thanks
to Minna Jung for her help
in the writing of this book.*

Hi, we're the **PONY TAILS**—May Grover, Corey Takamura, and Jasmine James. We're neighbors, we're best friends, and most of all, we're pony-crazy.

My name is **May.** My pony is named Macaroni after my favorite food, macaroni and cheese. He's the sweetest pony in the world! Jasmine and Corey say he's the exact opposite of me. Of course, they're just teasing. I have two older sisters who say I'm a one-girl disaster area, but they're not teasing. Would you like some used sisters? I have two for sale.

I'm called **Corey**—short for Corinne. I live between Jasmine and May—in a lot of ways. My house is between theirs. I'm between them in personality, too. Jasmine's organized, May's forgetful, and I can be both. May's impulsive, Jasmine's cautious, and I'm just reasonable. My pony is named Samurai. He's got a white blaze on his face shaped like a samurai sword. Sam is temperamental, but he's mine and I love him.

I'm **Jasmine.** My pony is named Outlaw. His face is white, like an outlaw's mask. He can be as unpredictable as an outlaw, too, but I'd never let him go to jail because I love him to pieces! I like to ride him, and I also like to look after him. I have a baby sister named Sophie. When she gets older I'm going to teach her to ride.

So why don't you tack up and have fun with us on our pony adventures!

May Corey Jasmine

JASMINE'S HOUSE

COREY'S HOUSE

MAY'S HOUSE

1 Mayday!

"I love the smell of autumn," announced May Grover. She had just walked out the back door of Jasmine James's house. May stopped and took a deep sniff.

Jasmine and Corey were right behind May. They bumped into her. May was usually ahead of the other two because she was always in a hurry to get where they were going. Now, though, they all stopped and admired the morning. The sky was a brilliant blue, the leaves were turning yellow and gold and red, and best of all, it was a Saturday—no school.

"I know what you mean," agreed

1

Corey. "Autumn smells like burning leaves, and wood smoke, and—"

"Apples! Autumn smells like apples!" interrupted May. Interrupting people was another habit of hers, but Corey and Jasmine were used to it. They were all best friends—and they knew May didn't mean to be rude. She was such a quick thinker, sometimes she couldn't wait to blurt out her ideas. That was what made her so much fun to be with, and what sometimes got her in trouble, too. Now her thoughts had jumped from autumn to apples!

"I love apples in the fall. They get redder, juicier, and sweeter," continued May. "I love eating them for snacks, and your mom, Jasmine, makes the best apple pie in the world."

Jasmine nodded proudly. Her mother was an artist. She was also an artist at baking. May and Corey often said that her mother's cookies were the best they'd ever tasted.

In the past week, Mrs. James had spent more time worrying than baking. Jasmine's baby sister, Sophie, was sick with a bad cold. Mr. and Mrs. James had even taken her to the hospital because they were concerned about her coughing. Now Sophie was better, and she and Mrs. James were sleeping. Jasmine's father, an ecologist, was working in his study. The whole house was quiet.

May and Corey had stopped by to pick up Jasmine on the way to Corey's stable. As they started walking over to Corey's house, May suddenly noticed something. "Oops, we left the back door open," she said. "I'll get it!"

May ran back and grabbed the doorknob. Unfortunately, she forgot about Jasmine's mother and sister. She swung the door shut with a loud slam. Immediately they all heard a terrible wail and then loud crying coming from upstairs. Sophie was awake—and that meant Mrs. James was awake, too.

"Oh no," said Jasmine softly. "Mom and Sophie haven't been sleeping very well lately."

"Jazz, I'm really sorry," began May. Before she could say anything else, the back door swung open. Mrs. James stood there, her hands on her hips, looking at

3

the girls. The expression on her face made May's heart sink.

"Mom, is Sophie okay?" asked Jasmine anxiously.

"Your father is trying to get her to sleep again," said Mrs. James. Then she shook her head tiredly. "Girls, how could you? You know Sophie's been sick all week. She needs her rest. I need my rest. Your father finally got a quiet moment to think and do some work. You can't just slam through a house like a tornado! You're old enough to behave more responsibly than that!"

All three friends were silent at first. Neither Jasmine nor Corey wanted to tell Mrs. James that May had slammed the door. They knew that May hadn't meant to wake up Sophie and Mrs. James. They also knew that May, once she had made a mistake, would always be brave enough to admit it. That was one of the things they liked best about her.

Sure enough, May stepped forward.

"Mrs. J., I slammed the door shut, and I'm sorry," she apologized. "I forgot about you and Sophie. Maybe," she added eagerly, "I can make up for it. I could

5

make you a cup of tea, or wash your car, or wash your windows, or something . . ."

Even though May was in trouble, Corey and Jasmine almost giggled. They couldn't picture May washing all the Jameses' windows!

Mrs. James did not seem to think it was funny. She just looked at May, then sighed. "Just please be quiet when Sophie's sleeping, May," she said. She turned and walked back into the house.

The three girls were quiet. Corey and Jasmine didn't feel like laughing anymore.

Then Jasmine turned to May. "She's really worried about Sophie," she said reassuringly. "You know Mom thinks you and Corey are the greatest."

May nodded, but she didn't smile back. Jasmine was right—normally, Mrs. James thought the world of the Pony Tails. Today she wasn't very happy with them.

The three girls called themselves the Pony Tails, because they were best friends and they loved ponies. They lived next door to each other, each of them had her own pony, and they all took riding lessons at the same stable, Pine Hollow. They also belonged to the same Pony Club—called Horse Wise because all the members wanted to learn as much as possible about horses and ponies.

On Saturdays, the girls usually had Horse Wise meetings. Mounted meetings meant they brought their own ponies from home. On weekdays, the girls' parents were too busy to bring their ponies, so the Pony Tails rode the ponies at Pine Hollow. At mounted meetings they practiced their riding skills. At unmounted meetings they learned all about taking care of their ponies.

This Saturday, though, Pine Hollow was closed. Max Regnery, the owner of the stable and the riding instructor for Horse Wise, had gone away on a trip to buy more horses and ponies.

The Pony Tails were disappointed about not going to Pine Hollow today. But they knew they could still have fun together. They knew they could do lots of things— ride their ponies, talk about ponies, or plan activities.

Most of the time, the three girls made a

great combination. May was a daredevil with crazy, fun ideas. Jasmine was always doing nice things for people and was patient with everyone. Corey's even temper and sense of humor kept everything in balance. The incident with Mrs. James, though, had darkened their moods considerably.

Corey poked May in the arm. "Come on," she said. "I wanted you and Jasmine to see this puppy that's staying at our barn. It's a really neat dog—I think you'll like it."

Then May smiled. The three started walking toward Corey's house, which stood between May's and Jasmine's homes. Corey and Jasmine didn't say anything else, but they both hoped that the day would get better for May.

Unfortunately, it didn't.

2 May's Day Gets Worse

The Pony Tails walked behind Corey's house, toward the big barn. Corey's mom was a veterinarian and was called Doc Tock—short for Dr. Takamura. May and Jasmine thought Corey's mom had one of the greatest jobs in the world. They could always find interesting animals in the Takamuras' barn.

First the Pony Tails said hello to Corey's pony, Samurai. Corey had named him for the white mark on his face, shaped like a samurai sword. When May and Jasmine had first met Corey, Samurai had been a very young pony, with a mind of his own that made him misbehave. He still had an independent spirit, but under Corey's patient guidance, he was getting better trained every day.

Corey took May and Jasmine to the back of the barn, where she often exercised Samurai in the big paddock attached to the barn. In a little fenced-off pen, they saw a small, slender puppy. He looked a bit like a fawn, with large, soft eyes and long, thin legs. His ears were much smaller than a fawn's, though, and were folded back against his head. He was mostly pale gray, with a little bit of black around his ears.

"Oooh," said May. Her face, which had been glum, immediately brightened. She climbed over the fence into the pen and knelt beside the dog. "What kind of a dog is this? He's so skinny! Does he eat enough?"

"It's a greyhound puppy," explained Corey. "His official name is Quicksilver, but we just call him Silver. He was supposed to go straight to CARL right after he got his shots, but he's so cute, I asked Mom if he could stay here a couple of extra days. Then he'll be put up for adoption at the shelter.

"And yes, he eats plenty!" she added with a laugh. "All greyhounds are skinny."

Corey, May, and Jasmine all knew that CARL—the County Animal Rescue League—would find a good home for Silver. CARL was committed to finding people who could adopt pets and really take care of them. The Pony Tails had helped Horse Wise raise money for CARL by riding their ponies in a horse show.

"I don't know if he's cute, exactly," said Jasmine. She reached down and touched Silver's head. His fur was so short and smooth that it hardly felt like fur at all.

The dog shivered a little but looked up at Jasmine trustingly. "He's so thin, and he has such long legs," observed Jasmine. "He looks kind of royal, doesn't he? Like a Thoroughbred horse."

"Thoroughbreds are racing horses, Jasmine!" laughed May. "Silver's legs look too skinny to even hold him up!"

"You wouldn't believe how fast greyhounds are," said a voice behind them. The three girls turned and saw Doc Tock smiling at them. She strolled over to the pen and bent down to pet Silver. "These dogs are sprinters—they can run short distances at incredible speeds. In fact," she added sadly, "its speed can be a greyhound's biggest problem."

"What do you mean, Mom?" asked Corey.

"Greyhound racing is a big business in some parts of the country," answered Doc Tock. "They run so quickly, some people think it's exciting to go to dog races and bet on which one will win. Most greyhounds, though, can only race at the top of their speed for about two or three years. They're just like racehorses—most horses only race about three or four years before they're retired. But greyhound owners don't bother to keep the dogs once they're older and aren't able to run as fast. They just . . . put them to sleep."

Corey, Jasmine, and May looked at Doc Tock in horror. The three girls didn't just love ponies—they loved all animals. This was one of the most awful things they had ever heard!

"Just because they can't run as fast as they used to?" May cried in disbelief. She put an arm protectively around Silver.

Doc Tock nodded. "In fact, most greyhounds are bred for racing only," she said. "If the puppies aren't quick enough, some of them get destroyed shortly after birth."

Seeing how upset the girls were, Doc Tock tried to reassure them. "Lots of people are trying to solve this problem," she said. "National organizations like the Greyhound Protection League are fighting to save these animals from being destroyed. They also try to outlaw greyhound racing, because then people won't have a reason to breed so many dogs.

"Also," she added, smiling down at Silver, "these organizations help find good homes for puppies like Silver or for dogs that have been retired from racing. Even though there are more dogs than available homes, every dog saved makes a difference. Greyhounds make good pets. They tend to be high-strung, but they're very gentle and intelligent."

Corey, May, and Jasmine all nodded. They knew that being "high-strung" was not necessarily bad. It just meant that the dogs might sometimes be nervous or sensitive. Horses and ponies were sometimes described as high-strung, too.

"I'm glad you're being adopted as a puppy," May said to Silver. He looked up at her and cuddled against her side. "Maybe I'll adopt a grown-up greyhound when I'm grown up," she added.

"They're really amazing dogs," said Doc Tock. "For example, they're visual hunters—which means that once they spot something moving, they chase it! They're so fast, they're gone just like that!"

Just then everyone heard a whinny from the barn. Corey laughed. "I think Sam wants us to visit him," she said. "And I think he wants me to bring him some hay!"

"I'll help you," said Jasmine.

"I'm going to stay here," said May. "I want to play some more with Silver."

14

Corey and Jasmine went inside the barn. Doc Tock went back to her office. With fewer people around, Silver became much livelier and playfully started chasing May around the pen. May began to understand how fast greyhounds could be. Silver was wearing her out—fast!

"Whew!" she finally puffed. "That's enough for me, Silver!"

As May lifted the latch of the pen's gate, she didn't notice that Silver was right behind her. She didn't notice, in fact, until he wriggled past her legs, ran through the gate, and dashed under the fence of the paddock!

"Oh no!" wailed May. She ran after Silver as fast as she could. She could still see him. He had stopped just at the edge of the field behind the Takamuras' paddock.

As May came closer, she saw Silver tilt his head. He seemed to be looking at something. When she got closer, she saw what it was—a little rabbit, about fifteen feet away from Silver.

Doc Tock's words flashed through May's mind: "Once they spot something moving, they chase it!" Sure enough, Sil-

ver darted after the rabbit, which ran across the field. Within a few seconds, Silver was out of sight in the woods beyond the field.

"Silver!" yelled May. She stopped to take a breath, panting. "Silver, come back! Silver! Si-i-l-l-l-verrrr! *Si-i-l-l-v-e-rrrr!*"

May kept on yelling at the top of her lungs, but Silver didn't appear. Unfortunately, Doc Tock did, followed by her student assistant, Jack Henry, and Corey and Jasmine. They had all heard May calling Silver.

"What happened?" asked Doc Tock. "How did Silver get out of his pen?"

May felt herself turn red with embarrassment. She had the sinking feeling that she was in trouble again—this time with Corey's mom. "I accidentally let him out, Doc Tock," she confessed. "I was leaving the pen, and—"

"Never mind, May," said Doc Tock impatiently. "Come on, Jack, we have to catch him."

Jack was already starting toward the woods. For more than an hour he and Doc Tock, assisted by the Pony Tails, chased

Silver. It wasn't easy. They would catch a glimpse of him and call his name, but then he would dodge away. He seemed to think they were playing a game!

Finally Jack made a terrific diving leap and managed to grab Silver. Once Silver was in Jack's arms, the dog wagged his tail and looked at them mischievously, as if to say, "What a lot of fun we just had!"

They all trudged back to the barn, exhausted. Doc Tock and Jack didn't say anything, and the girls were silent, too.

As they got closer to the paddock, May couldn't stay quiet any longer. "Doc Tock, I'm awfully sorry," she said. "I didn't know Silver would run away like that. I'll do anything to make up for letting him out. Maybe I can clean some cages, or feed the animals, or—"

"What's done is done," answered Doc Tock shortly. "Silver's not trained yet, and he should have stayed in his pen. I have several patients waiting for me in the office that could have been taken care of during this time. You," she said, looking at Corey, "can put Silver back in his pen. I have to get back to the office right away."

18

Jack handed Silver over to Corey, who held him carefully. Jack winked at May, as if to say he understood that she hadn't meant any harm—that it had all been an accident.

But May didn't see Jack wink. She was too upset. Normally Doc Tock was one of the friendliest moms in the world, taking an enthusiastic interest in everything the Pony Tails did. Now she was mad at May—just like Mrs. James was.

Corey and Jasmine wanted to comfort May, but they didn't know what to do or say. The three girls walked back to the paddock in silence.

What, thought May miserably, can go wrong next?

3 The Final Straw

After putting Silver in his pen and making sure the gate was securely fastened, the three girls headed over to May's house. They loved going to the Grovers' because Mr. Grover trained horses for a living and the Grovers' stable always had lots of horses in it.

Now they also wanted to go somewhere where no one was mad at May. May's face was so gloomy, Corey and Jasmine felt awful for her. They didn't know what to say.

When they walked into the Grovers' house, they found Mrs. Grover in the kitchen. May's mother loved horses and ponies, too, and could talk about them for hours.

Today, though, Mrs. Grover said a short hello to Corey and Jasmine. She didn't even smile at them, which was really strange. That was how they knew more trouble was coming.

"May," Mrs. Grover said sternly, "did you forget to tell me something?"

Mrs. Grover held out her hand. She was holding one of her shoes, except that it looked all wrong. The heel had broken off.

May slapped her forehead. "Mom, I forgot—"

Mrs. Grover interrupted her. "When I let you, Jasmine, and Corey try on my clothes yesterday, I thought you would be careful. Instead, I look for my favorite pair of dress shoes and find this." She waved the shoe back and forth angrily.

May, Jasmine, and Corey all looked at each other guiltily. Halloween was two weeks away, and the Pony Tails had thought that maybe they would dress up

as grown-ups this year. Mrs. Grover had agreed to let them try on some of her dresses, as long as they promised to be careful.

Trying on her dresses had been fun. They had spent an hour looking through her closet. Jasmine, who loved dolls and clothes much more than May or Corey, had been in heaven.

Both Jasmine and Corey remembered that May had been the one who had taken out Mrs. Grover's dress shoes and walked around in them. They also remembered that after the heel had broken, she had tried to put it back on with glue. Obviously, it hadn't worked.

Jasmine and Corey didn't want May to get in any more trouble. So Jasmine stepped forward and said, "Mrs. Grover, we're really sorry. We all wore the shoes. We did try to be careful. Maybe we can find some stronger glue and stick it back on—"

"No," interrupted May. She took a deep breath. "Don't try to cover up for me, Jazz. It was me," she told her mother. "I took out your shoes and walked around in

23

them until the heel broke off. I honestly thought I could fix it, but I know I was wrong to try them on in the first place."

Mrs. Grover shook her head. "That's not good enough, May. You promised me that you girls would be careful, and you broke that promise. You have to be punished. Go up to your room and stay there for one hour. You can see Jasmine and Corey later."

Jasmine and Corey looked at May sympathetically. She was bright red and looked as if she was going to cry. May almost never cried—she was the bravest one of the group. She didn't look at them, but turned and ran up to her room. Jasmine and Corey said good-bye to Mrs. Grover and left quietly.

In her room, May sniffed once but didn't cry. Although she felt miserable, she was almost relieved to be alone. "Now I can't make anyone else mad at me," she told herself. She lay down on her bed.

Mom is mad at me. Mrs. James is mad at me. Doc Tock is mad at me, she thought. What can I do about it? I already tried to apologize, but they wouldn't let me. I've got to find some way to make up for all the trouble I've caused.

Being in hot water was exhausting! Before she knew it, May had fallen fast asleep.

Outside, Jasmine and Corey walked slowly across the Grovers' lawn. "Poor May!" sighed Jasmine.

"Getting in trouble once is bad enough," said Corey. "But three times in one morning! She must be feeling awful."

"I don't think my mother is really that angry at her. I think she was just tired from taking care of Sophie," said Jasmine.

"I don't think my mother is, either. I think she was just tired from chasing Silver," said Corey.

"I wish there were something we could do," said Jasmine.

"Right now, I bet May just wants to be alone. Maybe we'll think of something later. I'm going home now," Corey said.

"Me too," Jasmine said. The two split up and headed toward their own houses.

When Corey got home, she poked her head into the office. She thought her mother might still be busy. But the waiting room was empty, except for Doc Tock and one person holding a cat. Doc Tock was handing the cat's owner some medicine.

When she saw Corey, she smiled. "Hey there," she called cheerfully. "I'm just about finished here. Just put these drops into his eyes three times a day for one week," she told the cat's owner. "Call me if there are any problems." Then she turned to Corey. "What say you and I take Silver over to CARL right now?"

Corey grinned. Lately her mother's veterinary practice had become very busy. Corey loved it when her mother could do something with her, just the two of them. "I guess the sooner we take him there, the sooner he can be adopted," she answered. "Is Jack coming, too?"

Doc Tock shook her head. "Jack has some small jobs to do around the office, and then he's going to feed and water the patients and go home. I'm going to spend some time at the shelter looking over the animals. Maybe you'd like to help?" She knew that Corey loved being around the animals at CARL.

"Check," said Corey, and ran to get a leash for Silver.

*   *   *

When Jasmine got home, she opened the back door very cautiously. She tiptoed into the kitchen.

"Bah bah bah," she heard. Her mom and dad and Sophie were in the kitchen. Mrs. James was just taking a tray of cookies out of the oven, and Sophie was lying in her baby seat, waving her arms around and gurgling happily.

Mrs. James looked at Jasmine with a smile. "Her fever's gone. She's feeling much better," she added with a laugh as Sophie broke into another stream of babble.

Jasmine sighed with relief. "Mom, I'm sorry about what happened earlier," she began.

Mr. James reached over and pulled Jasmine's blond braid affectionately. "Forget about it," he told her. "Sophie's feeling better, and that's all that counts for now. We've decided to go to Granny's house for a visit. She hasn't seen us for a while, because of all the craziness in the past weeks. How about it?"

"I'm taking these chocolate chip cookies over to Granny's for us all to share," added Mrs. James.

"Don't you have to work today?" asked Jasmine, looking at her father.

He shook his head. "All done—I'm all yours."

"All right!" said Jasmine happily. Granny was usually lots of fun!

4 When May Woke Up

When May woke up from her nap, she didn't know what time of day it was at first. Then she looked at the clock. "One o'clock!" she exclaimed. "I've been asleep for two hours!"

She sat up, rubbing her eyes. At first she felt fuzzy-headed. She almost never took naps in the middle of the day. She thought naps were for babies.

All the trouble today had wiped her out, though. As her brain slowly cleared, she remembered everything that had happened this morning. It was like waking up *to* a bad dream, instead of waking up *from* a bad dream, she decided.

Thinking about how Mrs. James, Doc Tock, and her own mother were all mad at her made May want to dive under the covers. But she knew hiding didn't solve anything. Maybe there was still something she could do to make up for all the trouble she'd caused. She got up, washed her face, and went downstairs.

The house was quiet. May wondered where her parents were, and whether her two older sisters, Ellie and Dottie, were around. When she wandered into the kitchen, she found her answer.

The Grovers were such a large and busy family, they kept track of each other's comings and goings on a large bulletin board in the kitchen. When May checked the board, the first thing she saw was a note from her parents. "May: We're doing some errands. It's 12:30 now and we'll be back in two hours." Then May saw another note from Ellie, saying that she was at soccer practice, and a note from Dottie, who was at a friend's house.

May realized she was alone in the house. She decided to call the other Pony Tails and see what they were doing.

Maybe they could come over and do something fun together. Or play with May's model ponies—Jasmine had the largest collection, but May had some nice ones, too.

Maybe she could save her Saturday after all.

First she called Jasmine. There was no answer. May hung up just as the machine came on. Maybe Jasmine was at Corey's.

She dialed Corey's number. Jack answered the phone.

"Oh, hi, Jack," said May. "Is Corey there?"

"Nope," he answered. "She and her mom went to take Silver over to CARL. They probably won't be back for a couple of hours."

"Thanks, Jack," said May. She hung up the phone. She wished that she had something to do and someone to do it with, but everyone seemed to be doing their own thing.

The phone rang. May picked it up. "Hello?" she said.

"May, is that you? It's Joey," said the voice.

May grinned. Joey Dutton used to live in Corey's house before he moved two towns away. May, Jasmine, and Joey had lived next door to each other for eight years. They were good friends, and Corey and Joey had gotten to meet and like each other, too.

Joey had his own pony, named Crazy. He used to ride at Pine Hollow, with Horse Wise, but now he rode with the Cross County Pony Club.

"Hi, Joey. Still feel bad about losing?" asked May jokingly.

"Just wait till next time," Joey joked back.

Now that Joey rode with another Pony Club, the friends sometimes saw one another at relay races between Horse Wise and Cross County. In the last relay race, Horse Wise had beaten Cross County. May couldn't resist teasing Joey a little, especially since she knew he was every bit as good a rider as the Pony Tails.

They talked for a few minutes. Then Joey said, "Listen, May. My dad came up with a great idea. There's an apple orchard right near Pine Hollow. The owners let you pick apples on horseback. Are the Pony Tails interested?"

May got excited. "I was just talking about how much I love apples, Joey," she said. "And so does Macaroni!" Macaroni was May's pony, named because of his yellow coat, mane, and tail, which reminded her of her favorite food, macaroni and cheese. He was so sweet and gentle, May liked the idea of giving him a special treat.

Plus, Joey and his dad were so much fun. Dr. Dutton, who was a dentist, had his own horse, named Ziggy. Ziggy had a goofy streak in him—just like Dr. Dutton!

May started thinking fast. Corey and Jasmine weren't home, but maybe they would come back in time to join May for part of the afternoon. She was dying to do something—and this sounded like the perfect something!

"Corey and Jasmine aren't around right now, but I am!" she told Joey. "When can we go?"

"Dad and I are at Pine Hollow right now," answered Joey. "We can ride over and pick you up in about forty-five minutes. Tell your parents we'll be back by five P.M."

"You bet," said May. She hung up the phone. Then she remembered that her parents were gone.

May felt a little uneasy about going apple-picking without telling her parents. But her parents knew Dr. Dutton and Joey well. They knew that May used to ride with them all the time. Also, May wasn't grounded anymore. Her hour of punishment was long over, and she was ready to have some fun. May felt sure that her parents would want her to go with Joey and Dr. Dutton.

After her morning of trouble, though, May decided not to take any chances. She ripped the last piece of paper from the message pad and wrote, "Dear Mom and Dad: I have gone apple-picking and riding with Joey and Dr. Dutton. I will be back at 5 P.M. Love, May." She pinned the note to the center of the bulletin board.

Then she called Corey's house. Jack answered the phone again.

"Jack, it's me, May, again," she said. "If

Corey comes back soon or if she calls in, can you please tell her where I'm going?"

"Sure, May, no problem," answered Jack. "Where *are* you going?"

"I'm going apple-picking with Joey Dutton and his dad. We're going to ride there," May told him. "The orchard is right near Pine Hollow. Corey can join me with Sam if she gets back in time. I'll be back at five P.M."

Just then, May heard a loud whimper in the background. "Is that Dracula?" she asked. She knew that Corey's dog often made weird howling noises, which was how he'd gotten his name.

"No," said Jack. "That's a German shepherd who's staying here. Broken leg. I thought he was fine, but he seems to be in a lot of pain. Listen, May, I have to go, okay?"

"Don't forget to give Corey my message," May reminded him.

"Um, no problem," Jack answered. He sounded distracted as he hung up the phone.

Then May called Jasmine to leave a

message on the machine. But when the machine picked up, she heard, "We're sssoooooooooorrrrry, grdlioup, leeeeave mrrrrrhhhh . . . *beep.*" Something was wrong with the Jameses' answering machine.

Since the machine had beeped, May began talking. "Jasmine, it's me, May. I'm going over to an apple orchard with Joey Dutton . . ." but then she stopped. All she heard from the machine was a lot of hissing and static. She became frustrated. "This is terrible!" she complained. "This isn't working—I give up!" She hung up the phone.

May walked out the back door and went to tack up Macaroni. May was good at tacking up ponies because she was around horses so much and she took care of Macaroni all by herself. All of the Pony Tails knew how to care for their own ponies.

She quickly put on Macaroni's saddle, fastened the girth snugly, and slipped the bridle over his head.

"This will be perfect, Macaroni," she told him. The pony nickered in response.

"I can go get bushels and bushels of sweet, ripe apples, and I'll give some to everyone. Maybe apples won't solve the problems I caused this morning, but at least people will know that I'm really sorry."

Macaroni snorted softly. May put her arms around his neck and hugged him. "You understand, don't you?" She led Macaroni out to the mounting block and swung into the saddle.

May could hardly wait to get going. She couldn't believe that she had just talked about apples this morning, and now she was going to eat all the apples she wanted.

What a fun way to make up for all the troubles of the morning! When she spotted Joey and Dr. Dutton riding Crazy and Ziggy, she tapped Macaroni gently with her heels. She said hello to the Duttons, and the three of them started off across the field in the direction of the orchard.

They were off to pick apples!

5 May's Messages Get Lost

It was just after three o'clock in the afternoon, Corey and Doc Tock weren't back from CARL yet, but the office was empty, and Jack had finished sweeping the floor. The phone rang, and he answered it.

"Hi, honey, guess what?" It was Jack's girlfriend, Kelly. She sounded pleased and excited. "A friend just gave me two tickets to the basketball game this afternoon. Can you get some time off from work today?"

Jack thought for a minute. The office was spotless, and he had fed and watered all the patients. The German shepherd with the broken leg had settled down after being given some medicine for his pain. He was now sleeping soundly.

"That sounds great, Kelly," Jack answered. "Sure, I can go. I've taken care of pretty much everything here." They made arrangements to meet, and he hung up.

As Jack walked out the door, he turned out the lights in the office. Just before he locked the door, he paused.

Was he forgetting something? He had a nagging feeling that there was something he had forgotten to do. Well, whatever it was, he could do it later.

Jack shut the door, making sure it was locked. Doc Tock had a lot of valuable equipment in her office. As he walked toward his car, he saw Ellie Grover walking up to the Grovers' front door. She was returning from soccer practice.

"Hey, Ellie," he called. He waved.

Ellie saw Jack and waved back.

As she walked through the front door, Ellie knew almost at once that no one was home. Normally the Grovers' house was a noisy, fun place. May often complained that you could go deaf in her house. Jasmine and Corey, whose homes were usually quiet if you didn't count Sophie's crying or animal noises, liked the chaos at the Grovers'.

Now it was totally quiet. Ellie tossed her gym bag on the floor and went to check the bulletin board.

The phone rang. It was Dottie.

"Hey, Ellie, is that you?" She sounded breathless, but Dottie often sounded that way. May joked that Dottie sounded excited because she thought about boys and nothing else. May, of course, didn't understand how anyone could prefer boys to ponies.

"Listen, Ellie, are Mom and Dad at home?" Dottie asked.

"No, just me," answered Ellie.

"Well, can you give them a message? I need to go over to the mall because Susan wants to get a pair of shoes, and Jane is coming with us, but Susan's dad can't pick us up, and Jane's mom and dad can't pick us up, but we need to be back by six because Bobby is going to call . . ."

"Hold on!" ordered Ellie. She was getting confused. "I need to write this down." She looked around for the message pad. Great! There was no paper left!

She looked around for a piece of paper or a napkin. She spotted May's note on the bulletin board. She pulled it off and, without reading it, turned it over and scribbled on the blank side, "Mom, Dad: Pick Dottie up at mall before 6."

"Got it," she told Dottie.

"Great, bye," said Dottie, and hung up.

Just as Ellie hung up, the phone rang again. It was her friend Sandy.

"Ellie, I need you right away!" Sandy sounded very dramatic. "David Richter just asked me out to the movies tonight, and I have no idea what to wear!"

"I'll be right over," promised Ellie. She was happy for Sandy, who had liked David Richter for some time. She wrote on Dottie's message, "Gone to Sandy's. Be back soon. Love, Ellie." She pinned the note back on the bulletin board.

As she walked down the block to Sandy's, Ellie suddenly paused. Hadn't there been a note on the other side of the piece of paper? She remembered seeing

May's name on it, but she'd forgotten to read it.

Ellie shrugged. It was only a note from May. She was probably off with the other Pony Tails, doing their usual unimportant stuff.

Sandy was waiting. Now, *that* was important!

6 More Signals Get Crossed

Macaroni tossed his head. The day was beautiful. The sun was shining, and the air was cool and crisp. May could tell that Macaroni was having a wonderful time. He picked up his feet briskly as he trotted and swished his tail.

May, Joey, and Dr. Dutton were having a wonderful time, too. The apple farm was a couple of miles from May's house, and the ride, so far, was as much fun as May had hoped.

The three of them were laughing and talking. Dr. Dutton told May that he had packed a little picnic for them in his saddlebag, "just to keep our strength up for picking apples."

When they got to the farm, May saw a sign, SUSAN'S APPLE ORCHARD: PICK YOUR OWN. Cars were pulled up in front of the main barn. At the barn, people were either picking up baskets to go and pick apples, or weighing the apples they had just picked.

Behind the barn, the Duttons and May could see rows and rows of apple trees. "Look, some other people are on horseback, too," said Joey. But May only had eyes for one thing.

"Look at the apples!" she exclaimed. She could see the shiny red apples peeking out from the branches. Some of the branches were bent over with the weight of apples.

May turned to Joey and Dr. Dutton. "Let's go!" she urged them.

Dr. Dutton laughed. "Not so fast, May," he said, grinning. "Remember our lunch? You want to let this poor old dentist starve?"

May chuckled. Dr. Dutton loved to eat.

He used to make the best hamburgers when the Duttons lived next door to May and Jasmine. The three families would often barbecue together, and Dr. Dutton even made super-special veggie burgers for Jasmine's family.

"Besides, we can pick apples for dessert," added Dr. Dutton.

May felt a rumble in her stomach. After all, she had skipped lunch because she had fallen asleep during her punishment. If she knew Dr. Dutton and Joey, they had packed something yummy.

"How about there?" she said, pointing to a grove of trees near the back of the barn.

"Great," agreed Joey and Dr. Dutton. They tethered Ziggy, Crazy, and Macaroni to the trees, then sat down on a blanket that Dr. Dutton had brought.

May was glad they had stopped to eat, especially when Dr. Dutton produced hero sandwiches, potato chips, and apple juice from his saddlebag. May ate her sandwich in record time.

"Save room for dessert, May!" warned Joey. "Apples, remember?"

"How could I forget?" answered May. She looked longingly at the apple trees, then jumped up and walked over to Macaroni. She patted his nose and said, "Just you wait, Mac. Soon you'll be eating all the apples you want."

"An apple a day keeps the doctor away," said Dr. Dutton.

"What about dentists?" asked Joey. They all laughed.

*   *   *

"I can't believe Silver already found a new home!" said Corey happily.

Doc Tock smiled at Corey as they pulled up to the house. They had just gotten home from CARL. Doc Tock had examined all the animals at the shelter, and Corey had helped her mother and played with some of the animals, too.

Best of all, Silver had been spotted by a family immediately and picked for adoption. Both Doc Tock and Corey had chatted with Silver's new family and had liked them very much.

As soon as she got home, Corey scrambled out of the car. She wanted to call May and tell her about it. Maybe the news would cheer her up.

When she dialed the Grovers' number, there was no answer. Corey wondered where May was, and thought she might be with Jasmine. She called Jasmine's number.

Jasmine answered the phone. "Hello?" she said. Her voice sounded funny.

Corey frowned. "Jasmine, what's wrong? You sound weird."

Jasmine was silent for a second, then blurted out, "Oh, Corey, I'm so scared. I think May's in trouble."

Corey was surprised. "What do you mean, in trouble? Like this morning?"

"No," answered Jasmine. "We just got home from Granny's, and there was a message from May. The message sounded really strange, Corey. There was a lot of crackling and static. We couldn't understand what May was saying at first. Then we heard her say, 'This is terrible! This isn't working—I give up!'"

Corey tried to think. What could May have been talking about? "Do you think

May is still upset about what happened this morning?'' she asked Jasmine.

"That's what I'm so worried about,'' said Jasmine. "After all, she had a terrible morning. I know that I would be really up-set if I were in her place. I just called her, but there was no answer.''

"I just tried, too,'' Corey told her. "May *should* be home, though—I thought she was grounded, remember? Let's go over and see if she's there.''

"Meet you outside,'' answered Jasmine.

When the two girls met outside, Corey tried to reassure Jasmine. "I'm sure May just fell asleep or something,'' she told her. "Otherwise, she definitely would pick up the phone. She was probably still upset when she called you.''

Jasmine nodded but didn't say anything. She looked worried.

When they got to the Grovers', the two girls went around to the back. In their neighborhood, people rarely locked their back doors when they went away for short periods.

The Grovers' door was unlocked, and they walked into the kitchen.

"May?" called Jasmine.

"Mrs. Grover? Mr. Grover?" called Corey.

No one answered. "What about the bulletin board?" suggested Corey. They knew that the Grovers left messages for one another there.

"Look, here's one about Ellie and Dottie," said Jasmine.

"And one from May's parents," added Corey.

The two girls looked at each other. "Where's May?" they said at the same time.

Usually when the Pony Tails said the same thing at the same time, they would give each other a high five, then a low five, and then say, "Jake!" Now they were too concerned about May to do it.

Jasmine started toward the staircase. "I'm going to check her room," she said determinedly. "Maybe she's asleep, but I want to find out if she's okay."

"I'm coming, too," said Corey, following her.

When they got to May's room, the two girls found it empty. The room looked

50

much the same as always—posters of ponies on the walls, messy bed—except no May. Then Corey noticed something.

"Look, May's riding boots are gone!" she cried out.

Jasmine turned to look. "Her hard hat is gone, too!" She and Corey looked at each other.

May *never* went riding by herself. She always rode with her friends or with an adult because it wasn't safe to ride alone. But if the Grovers were out doing errands, and Corey and Jasmine had just gotten back, what did that mean? Had May gone riding all by herself?

"Let's check the stable," Corey said to Jasmine. They ran out of the house.

7 The Mystery of May's Disappearance

Normally Corey and Jasmine liked visiting the Grovers' stable. They usually stopped and patted Hank, the oldest horse there. They would stop and chat with Dobbin, Mr. Grover's bay gelding, who was the most curious horse in the stable. They also liked to see the other horses Mr. Grover kept there for training.

Today, Corey and Jasmine ran straight to Macaroni's stall. Empty!

"Macaroni's gone!" exclaimed Jasmine in dismay.

"Oh no!" cried Corey at the same time.

The two of them stared at one another. "Maybe," said Jasmine very slowly, "May couldn't get over what happened this morning. Maybe she wanted to get away."

"What are you saying?" asked Corey. "Do you think May has run away from home?"

Jasmine nodded.

Corey thought about what had happened that morning. May had gotten in trouble before. Most of the time, she would apologize and everything would be okay. Today, May had gotten in trouble three times!

"She must feel like *everyone* is mad at her," Corey said.

Jasmine's eyes were beginning to fill with tears. But then she turned around and headed for the stable door. "Come on, Corey, we have to find her," she said. "I'm going to go get Outlaw." Outlaw was Jasmine's pony, named for the bandit mask on his face. "You tack up Sam," she added, "and we'll meet in front of my house and go and look for May."

Corey began to follow Jasmine, but then she stopped short. "Wait, Jasmine," she advised. "I'm worried about May, too.

But we know we're not allowed to ride off by ourselves without permission. Our parents told us that was dangerous."

"You're right," said Jasmine. "But then what do we do?"

"We get our parents," said Corey firmly. "They'll know what to do. Come on—let's go to your house first."

*　　*　　*

May stretched her arm as far as she could. If she could just reach a little farther . . .

There! Her fingers touched a round, red, shiny apple. She pulled it off the branch and placed it in one of the bags hooked onto her saddle. The owners of the orchard had provided special pairs of paper bags for horse and pony riders that went over the pony's back and hung down on each side. They were just like real Western saddlebags.

"I couldn't do this without your help," May told Macaroni. She patted his mane. "When I'm riding you, I'm so much taller. I can reach the best apples that way!"

Macaroni reached down and sniffed at an apple on the ground. May, Joey, and Dr. Dutton had already let Ziggy, Crazy, and Macaroni eat their ration of windfalls by removing their bits for a while. Now Macaroni was full of delicious apples, but May wasn't finished picking.

"Your bags are getting pretty full, May!" called Joey from under another tree.

"I'm not finished yet!" she called back. She was having a great time. Joey was picking a lot of apples, too, and Dr. Dutton was clowning around, picking apples but pretending to fall off Ziggy.

The afternoon had turned warmer with golden sunshine, and the scent of the apples was everywhere. May was picking only the reddest, ripest apples. She wanted to give her mother, Doc Tock, and Mrs. James the best.

It was impossible to be miserable on this beautiful fall day. The troubles of the morning seemed to have melted away. May knew that she had caused a lot of problems, but she thought that once everyone saw the gifts she had brought them, all would be forgiven.

May also knew that she had been extra-careful about letting her family and friends know where she was and when she was going to be back. She had gotten into trouble in the past by rushing off to do something with the Pony Tails and not letting her parents know where she was. "But this time, I did everything right," she told herself. "Nobody is getting upset because of me."

She reached up and picked another apple. The owners of the orchard urged people to try a few apples for themselves before paying for the ones they had picked. There were plenty to go around.

May rubbed the apple clean on her shirt, took a bite, and sighed with pleasure. It was perfect—crisp, juicy, and sweet. "Having a good time, May?" asked Dr. Dutton, riding by on Ziggy.

"The greatest!" answered May. It was true.

8 Back Home

Mr. and Mrs. Grover pulled the grocery bags out of the car. They shut the car doors and walked toward the house.

The errands had taken them a little longer than Mrs. Grover had expected. "I wonder if May's still asleep?" she said. She had peeked in on May before they'd left.

Then Mrs. Grover suddenly stopped and stared. "What are Doc Tock and Corey doing on our lawn?" she asked.

Mr. Grover stopped, too. "What are the Jameses doing here?" he demanded to know.

When the group on the lawn spotted the Grovers, they all started speaking at once. "It was my fault," began Mrs. James.

"No, it was mine," chimed in Doc Tock. Corey and Jasmine started talking at the same time.

"Wait just a minute!" yelled Mr. Grover. He didn't mean to yell, but he couldn't understand a word anyone was saying.

"Can someone please tell us what is going on?" asked Mrs. Grover, more quietly.

"May is missing. We think she's run away," said Corey bluntly. "We looked for her everywhere, and Macaroni's missing, too. Last time we saw May, she was really upset. And Jasmine got a strange message from May on their machine."

"Did you check the bulletin board?" asked Mrs. Grover. Corey and Jasmine nodded.

Quickly the Grovers were filled in on all the details. Mrs. Grover dropped her grocery bag and put a hand to her forehead. Mr. Grover looked worried.

Mrs. James stepped forward. "It's my

fault," she told the Grovers. "I shouldn't have gotten so angry at May for slamming the door. I knew it was just an accident. Sophie is fine now. I shouldn't have lost my temper. I'm the reason May ran away."

Doc Tock shook her head. "No, it's my fault," she said. "May didn't know Silver could run like that. She didn't mean to let him out of the pen. She tried to apologize for what she did, but I wouldn't let her. I shouldn't have treated her that way."

"No," said Mrs. Grover. She looked very upset. "I was the one who punished May. I was angry because they were my favorite dress shoes, but those heels were starting to wobble long before May tried them on. I might have broken that heel off myself if I had worn them again. I can't believe I yelled at her."

"We were all wrong," said Mrs. James.

Doc Tock and Mrs. Grover nodded in agreement.

"We all got tired, and careless, and lost our tempers when we didn't need to," said Doc Tock.

"While I was running errands, I bought

May a little something to make up for it," Mrs. Grover told the group.

Mrs. James began to smile. "On the way back from Granny's, I bought something for May, too."

They both looked at Doc Tock. She smiled and said, "Guilty—I bought May a little something on the way back from CARL—"

"Here, now," Mr. Grover broke in. "We can't just stand around talking. We need to find May. I'm going to try and find her trail, because I'm sure she rode across the field. I'm going to saddle Dobbin right now."

The mothers began to look worried again. Corey and Jasmine, however, ran to Mr. Grover. "Can we come, too?" they begged. "Please let us help!"

"Okay," agreed Mr. Grover. "Go tack up your ponies, girls. I'll wait for you by our stable."

Mrs. Grover turned to Mrs. James and Doc Tock. "Why don't we wait in our kitchen until we hear some news?" she suggested. "I'll make a pot of coffee." She picked up her bag of groceries again.

Mrs. James and Doc Tock picked up the groceries Mr. Grover had dropped and followed Mrs. Grover into the house.

*   *   *

"I think it's time to weigh our apples, don't you?" asked Dr. Dutton.

May's bags were almost overflowing. In fact, she was afraid they would break. But she was tremendously excited—she had picked more than enough for Mrs. James, Doc Tock, and her mother. She had eaten three of the delicious apples, and each one had tasted better than the last.

Macaroni seemed to think so, too. He was practically acting drunk from eating so many windfalls! As for Ziggy and Crazy, both of them were prancing like little foals again.

May and the Duttons took their apples to the main barn, where scales were set up for weighing them. Dr. Dutton took out his wallet to pay for the apples, but May stopped him. "I can pay for mine, Dr. Dutton," she told him, digging into her pocket. "I brought my allowance savings."

"Are you sure, May?" Dr. Dutton asked. "After all, you picked a lot of apples!"

"Yeah, did you leave any apples in the orchard for other people?" joked Joey.

May made a face at Joey. "There are more than enough apples for everyone," she declared. "And I *am* sure—I want to pay for these apples all by myself, because I'm giving most of them away as presents. I need," she added, "to make up for something I did."

Dr. Dutton ruffled May's hair approvingly. May's bags were set on the scale. She had the heaviest harvest of the three of them!

May felt proud. For a day that had started out so badly, this one was turning out to be just about perfect.

Dr. Dutton started slinging the bags over the saddles. "Keep on checking yours, May," he warned. "You have so many, I'm afraid the bags will break."

May promised to be careful. The three riders started for home. The ride there

had taken about a half hour. May had promised to be home by five P.M. The sun slanted across the fields—it was getting lower in the sky.

May sighed with happiness. "What a beautiful day," she said.

Dr. Dutton and Joey agreed wholeheartedly. All three of them were starting to feel tired, but the afternoon had been worth it.

9 The Search Continues

Mr. Grover led the way, riding his bay gelding, Dobbin. Corey and Jasmine followed him, heading toward the field behind the Grovers' stable.

Outlaw and Samurai were behaving unusually well. Sometimes Outlaw could be frisky and temperamental. Samurai, too, was known for occasionally being disobedient. But today Outlaw and Samurai were behaving perfectly. It was as if they knew that Corey and Jasmine needed their cooperation.

It was impossible to tell, from the field behind the Grovers' stable, where May and Macaroni had gone. The field was full of horse and pony tracks. Mr. Grover shook his head in frustration.

"Maybe May headed over to Pine Hollow," suggested Corey. They rode in that direction.

Mr. Grover suddenly stopped Dobbin and dismounted. He peered at the ground. "There are tracks here, but they seem to have been made by one horse and two ponies. See, you can tell which ones are the horse's tracks. They're larger and deeper."

Corey and Jasmine bent down for a closer look. "These look like they were made by three horses," suggested Corey, pointing at another spot.

"And these look like they were made by three ponies," said Jasmine, pointing to another set of tracks. "I think those were the tracks we made when we went riding yesterday."

Mr. Grover looked even more frustrated. "Two ponies, one horse, three ponies—but no tracks made by one pony with one girl! Where can May have gone?"

"We have to keep on searching," urged

Corey. Mr. Grover got back on Dobbin, and the three of them continued riding toward Pine Hollow.

Jasmine and Corey rode a little way behind Mr. Grover. They could tell he was worried. So were they.

"Are you thinking what I'm thinking?" Jasmine asked Corey softly.

"I'm thinking about where May could be," answered Corey.

"Me too," sighed Jasmine. "I'm scared that we won't find her," she added.

"Of course we'll find her," said Corey. But her voice didn't sound as firm and reasonable as it usually did.

Jasmine continued talking. "I keep on thinking that maybe we could have stopped this from happening," she said to Corey.

"How?" asked Corey. "We didn't break the heel off Mrs. Grover's shoe. We didn't slam the door. We didn't let Silver out of his pen."

"Yes, but we *know* May," explained Jasmine. "We're her best friends. We know that she sometimes doesn't think before she acts. We know that she makes mistakes. So do we! Isn't that part of being someone's friend? That you can help your friend *not* make a mistake?"

Corey nodded solemnly. "I didn't think of that, Jasmine, but you're right," she said. "We love May because she has such great ideas and is ready for anything. But we could also help her think ahead."

Jasmine said, "I could have closed the door, or reminded her to be quiet."

"I could have warned her to be extra-careful with Silver," said Corey.

"Maybe we should have tried to talk to her more after she got in trouble," said Jasmine.

"We didn't really try hard enough to comfort her," said Corey.

Corey and Jasmine looked at each other, appalled. Maybe they were to blame for May's disappearance!

"Mom always says you can't cry over spilt milk," said Corey suddenly.

"What does that mean?" asked Jasmine.

"Mom says it means you can't undo mistakes you've already made. And it's no good to just sit around and worry about them, either," said Corey. "All you can do is try and not make the same mistakes again. And that means that we have to find May and be better friends to her from now on."

Jasmine nodded. "You're right," she said.

As they rode on, though, Jasmine couldn't help imagining where May was now. Jasmine was very softhearted, and she had a vivid imagination. She remembered May's expression when she ran upstairs after being punished by Mrs. Grover.

Jasmine began to picture May, all alone with Macaroni. Maybe she was already starting a new life. Maybe she had changed her name. Maybe she had changed Macaroni's name. That would make them so much harder to find! Jasmine started thinking about names that May might use. "June and Spaghetti?" she wondered out loud.

Corey didn't hear Jasmine. She, too, was getting more upset about May. She thought that May must be feeling very alone and scared right now. She pictured

May riding Macaroni along a lonely road. What would she do for food? Where would she and Macaroni sleep at night?

Maybe, thought Corey, May would have to figure out ways of making money. Maybe she would be forced to sell pony rides on Macaroni for a living. Maybe she and Macaroni would join a circus!

Poor May! Corey and Jasmine thought.

*   *   *

"Poor May!" said Joey. He was only joking, though. He was teasing May because he thought she had too many apples in her bags.

"What are you going to do if the bags break, May?" asked Dr. Dutton. "Are you going to carry them in your cheeks, the way a squirrel does with nuts?"

"Don't feel sorry for me!" May told Joey, laughing. "I picked more apples than anybody today, and I need them all! The bags have just *got* to hold together until I get home!"

The sun was definitely getting lower in the sky. May could tell that it was close to five P.M., the time she had said she would be home. As they rode back, she got more and more excited. She could hardly wait to give the apples away. She planned to keep a few for herself, but most of her harvest would go to her mother, Mrs. James, and Doc Tock. Mrs. James could make applesauce for Sophie. Doc Tock could snack on apples while she worked. May's mom could make apple crisp with vanilla ice cream, one of the Grovers' favorite desserts.

May could tell that Macaroni was getting tired. He had done a lot of good work that day and needed to be fed and watered. "Just a few minutes more, Mac," she said, patting him.

They were almost home!

*　　*　　*

"That's enough, girls," said Mr. Grover. "We shouldn't be riding when the sun starts to go down. The horses can't see as well, and they might stumble on a rock or a hole. We have to quit for now."

Corey turned Sam around, and Jasmine

did the same with Outlaw. With Dobbin leading the way, the three riders headed toward the Grovers' home. They were tired and discouraged, and most of all, they were really worried about May.

The sky was just starting to turn red and gold with the beginnings of sunset. Jasmine looked across the field and saw the Grovers' stable clearly.

Just then Corey cried out, "Look!" She pointed across the field.

Coming across the field were three riders, one on a horse and two on ponies. Mr. Grover let out a shout. "May!" he called. "Is that you?"

*   *   *

Back in the Grovers' kitchen, Mrs. Grover had just put on another pot of coffee. She, Mrs. James, and Doc Tock had tried to make conversation with each other. But they kept on lapsing into silence. They were all too concerned about May.

Finally Mrs. Grover got up and restlessly wandered to the kitchen window. "I

wonder if they've found anything," she said. Then she gave a start.

"Look!" She pointed out the window.

Mrs. James and Doc Tock rushed over to join her and saw, in the field behind the Grovers' stable, two sets of three riders coming across the field from opposite directions. Both sets of riders were headed toward the Grovers'.

Mrs. Grover turned off the coffeepot and rushed outside. On her heels were Mrs. James and Doc Tock.

The six riders arrived at the Grovers' paddock at the same time. The mothers were eagerly waiting for them there. Everything became very confused and noisy, with everyone trying to talk at once.

"May, why did you do it?" cried Mrs. James.

"May, I'm sorry for getting so angry with you," said Doc Tock.

"May, I shouldn't have punished you," said Mrs. Grover.

"May, we're really sorry," said Corey and Jasmine together.

"*Hold it!*" yelled May. Everyone became quiet.

"Why is everyone apologizing?" asked May. "What's going on here?"

Mrs. Grover ran over to Joey and Dr. Dutton, who were still on horseback. "Thank you so much for finding May," Mrs. Grover said. She reached up and grabbed Dr. Dutton's hand to shake it.

"How did you know she had run away?" asked Mrs. James. "You two are geniuses!"

Joey and Dr. Dutton looked completely baffled. "I always thought I was pretty smart, but a genius?" Dr. Dutton began to joke. Then he looked at everyone's serious face and stopped.

Then Joey and Dr. Dutton looked at May for an explanation.

"What is everyone talking about?" asked May, totally bewildered. "I just went apple-picking with Joey and Dr. Dutton!"

Mrs. Grover stepped back. She leaned against a fence rail. "You just went apple-picking with Joey and Dr. Dutton?" she repeated. "But why didn't you tell us you were going? We were worried sick!"

May was surprised. She began to explain that she had left messages with everyone.

But as she tried to explain what had happened, she realized that no one—not a single person!—had gotten her messages!

"Uh-oh," said May. She had a sinking feeling that she was in trouble again. This time she had done everything she was supposed to, but everyone was still mad at her!

Ellie strolled up and joined the group. She had just returned from Sandy's house. "Hi, what's the commotion?" she asked casually.

"May was gone for the entire afternoon. Everyone thought she had run away," her mother told her. "No one knew where she was!"

"I left a message on the bulletin board!" insisted May.

Ellie looked at her mother. Then she looked at May. Then she slowly closed her eyes. "Oh boy, I've really done it," she said.

"What are you talking about? What does this have to do with you, Ellie?" Mr. Grover asked.

"Follow me," was all Ellie would say.

First of all, the six riders dismounted and tied Ziggy, Dobbin, and the four ponies to the paddock fence. When they went to the kitchen, they found Ellie showing the note she had scribbled on to her mother, Mr. and Mrs. James, and Doc Tock. Sure enough, on the other side they found May's message about apple-picking.

Then Doc Tock called her answering service, which took messages when she and Jack weren't in the office. "I have a message from Jack, saying that he forgot to leave a note that May had gone apple-picking with Joey Dutton and his father," she announced.

"And then I tried to call Jazz and tell her, but the answering machine was broken," finished May. "I got frustrated and hung up!"

Everyone was silent for a whole minute. The events of the afternoon, as they had really happened, were just starting to sink in.

Then everyone started to laugh. Mr. and Mrs. Grover hugged May. Corey and

Jasmine also hugged her, and told her how scared they had been. Mr. and Mrs. James and Doc Tock first hugged May, then hugged their own daughters.

No one was mad at May anymore. Mrs. Grover asked her, "Did you have a good time?"

May nodded enthusiastically. "It was the best!" she said. "We had a picnic lunch. I got to pick apples on horseback. I ate apples. Macaroni ate a ton of apples. We had an amazing time!"

"Wow!" said Corey and Jasmine enviously at exactly the same time. They turned to each other and said, "Jake!" and gave each other a low five and a high five. May's day sounded like a blast!

"I have a surprise for all the moms," announced May. She ran outside. A minute later she returned, lugging her bags of apples. "I picked tons and tons of apples for everyone!" she told them.

The mothers exclaimed at how red and beautiful the apples were. May got busy dividing the apples among Mrs. Grover, Mrs. James, and Doc Tock.

"I wanted to show you that I was really,

truly sorry for all the trouble I caused this morning," she told the three of them. "And I want you to know that I've made a very important decision today."

"What's that?" asked Mr. Grover, one eyebrow slightly raised.

"I've decided never, ever to get in trouble again!" declared May.

The three moms smiled. Then Mrs. Grover spoke.

"No one expects you to never, ever get in trouble, May," she said. Everyone laughed. They all knew May!

"What we do expect is that you try to think carefully," Mrs. Grover continued. "But we owe you an apology, too, May. I've talked this over with Jasmine's mom and Corey's mom, and we all feel as if we flew off the handle. My shoe will be fine, Sophie is fine, and Silver is fine. We shouldn't have gotten so angry with you, and we're sorry for making your day begin so miserably. I'm glad, though, that you made up for it at the apple orchard. And I'm especially glad"—she gave May another hug—"for all these delicious apples!"

"Me too," said Mrs. James.

"Me three!" said Doc Tock.

The three moms paused. There was a short silence, which started to get awkward. The Pony Tails looked at each other in confusion. What was going on here?

"Didn't you say you had gotten a little something for May?" Mrs. Grover asked Mrs. James.

Mrs. James shrugged and turned to Doc Tock. "Didn't you say you'd brought her a little gift?" she asked.

Doc Tock chuckled and pointed to Mrs. Grover. "You first," Doc Tock said.

Mrs. Grover grinned. "Okay, I'll go first," she said. "While everyone was out looking for May and Macaroni, the moms discovered that we had something new in common!" She reached under the kitchen table, brought out a basket, and gave it to May.

"For you, May," Mrs. Grover told her. May looked inside the basket. Nestled inside were five bright, shiny, redder-than-red apples!

"I knew how much you love apples, and I thought you might like these!" laughed Mrs. Grover.

"We got you apples, too," chimed in Mrs. James and Doc Tock. They, too, brought out baskets of red, shiny apples and gave them to May.

May looked at the three little baskets of beautiful apples. Then she turned and looked at the enormous, bulging bags of apples she had just picked for her mother, Mrs. James, and Doc Tock.

Then she started to giggle.

Corey and Jasmine giggled too. Joey, and all the parents, joined in the girls' laughter.

They were relieved that May was safe at home. They were happy that her day had ended so well. All three of the Pony Tails had done something fun on their Saturday. Next Saturday, they would all go to Horse Wise and learn more about ponies—together.

Then May reached into her brand-new baskets of apples and began handing them around.

"There's no such thing as too many apples!" she said, taking a bite out of one.

The kitchen filled with crunching noises. Everyone agreed.

MAY'S TIPS FOR PONY FUN

I know it seems silly to tell you how to have fun with your pony. Personally, I start having fun the minute I *think* about Macaroni. I have fun when I'm working with him. I even have fun when I'm working *for* him. Not that I exactly love mucking out stalls, but anything that's good for Macaroni is fun because I love him so much.

What I want to tell you about is how to have *more* fun on your pony when you're not in a class. The first step in having more fun is using your imagination. We all know about riding in circles in a ring and taking a class. Some of us are lucky enough to be able to take trail rides with friends. Those are great things to do, but they're just a start.

Apple picking with Joey and his dad is an example of what a little imagination can do for you. If you can do it outdoors, on foot, you can do it on a pony. Mostly. Um, maybe. Okay, well, softball is out of the question, but there's a game that's a mixture of polo and lacrosse called polocrosse that you play on ponies. See what I mean? Somebody was using her imagination. You can use yours, too.

One of the Pony Tails' favorite things to do is to go on a trail ride that isn't just a trail ride. It's a picnic! When we were littler, we had to have a grown-up with us. That was okay, but it's more fun alone. One day our parents finally decided that if there were three of us going (so that one could always go for help), and if we didn't go too far (we had to be able to hear my dad ring the bell behind our house), *and* if we didn't stay too long (one hour), *and* if we borrowed Doc Tock's cellular phone, then we could go on a picnic. That's a lot of *if*s and *and*s, but it's worth all of them. Picnics are fun, being with friends is fun, and riding is fun. Put them all together and it's a blast!

The only thing that's better than a picnic is camping out. How about doing that with your pony? That makes camping out even better. Pine Hollow has a camping trip every year called the Mountain Trail Overnight. I sure hope our parents will decide that we're old enough to go this year. I can't wait. But in the meantime, Dad took the three of us on a camp-out last summer. It was great—until the mosquitoes decided they hadn't had enough dinner and started using us for dive-bombing practice. We all came home about two o'clock in the morning! Fortunately, my sisters were asleep, so they couldn't make fun of us.

One of the things the Pony Tails can always do when we're riding is to play pretend games. Sometimes we play horse—I mean *pony*—show. We take turns competing at the National Horse Show, and last week I won a gold medal at the Olympics!

With my imagination, I can make anything happen. I can create a fairyland (Jasmine's favorite); we can go on a treasure hunt (Corey's choice); or we can hunt down the varmints who robbed the bank (guess who likes that one?). Sometimes we go on imaginary trips, too. One day we're in the Arabian desert; the next day we're watching out for deadly snakes in a tropical forest. There was a time when my imagination took me along with a group exploring an ancient Mayan tomb. I screamed when they took the cover off the coffin. Unfortunately, I was really at a Pony Club meeting, and it was hard to explain to Max what had happened. That's what my father calls "the downside of a vivid imagination."

So go ahead, have some fun. It'll make you feel just like one of the Pony Tails!

About the Author

Bonnie Bryant was born and raised in New York City, and she still lives there today. She spends her summers in a house on a lake in Massachusetts.

Ms. Bryant began writing about girls and horses when she started The Saddle Club series in 1987. So far there are more than sixty books in that series. Much as she likes telling the stories about Stevie, Carole, and Lisa, she decided that the younger riders at Pine Hollow Stables, especially May Grover, have stories of their own. That's how Pony Tails was born.

Ms. Bryant rides horses when she has time away from her computer, but she doesn't have a horse of her own. She likes to ride different horses, enjoying a variety of riding experiences. She thinks most of her readers are much better riders than she is!